This Little Tiger book

belongs to:

_____

_____

_____

For Grandpa Len ~ S S
For Arthur ~ R W

LITTLE TIGER PRESS
1 The Coda Centre
189 Munster Road, London SW6 6AW
www.littletiger.co.uk

First published in Great Britain 2014
This edition published 2014
Text copyright © Steve Smallman 2014
Illustrations copyright © Richard Watson 2014
Steve Smallman and Richard Watson have asserted their rights
to be identified as the author and illustrator of this work
under the Copyright, Designs and Patents Act, 1988

ISBN 978-1-84895-750-3
Printed in China
LTP/1400/0971/0714
2 4 6 8 10 9 7 5 3

Grumpy Branch

It was a dreamy, sunbeamy day
in Cupcake Wood.

Birds sang sweetly. Bunnies hopped
happily. And a big, brown, bumbling bear
was doing what bears do in the woods.

Everyone was happy. Everyone except...

...Scowl.

Too white!

He was even grumpy
in his sleep.

Grumpy Branch

The other animals decided
that **Scowl** needed cheering up.
One little bird had
a great idea.

"You can wear my HAPPY HAT!"
she twittered, plonking it on Scowl's head.

said **Scowl.**

"I'll sing **Scowl** my happy song!" said a fluffy little bunny.

"I'm a happy **hoppy** bunny, yes I am!"

I am!

"I'm as jolly as a pot of strawberry jam!"

I am!

"I'm a happy little **poppet** and I never want to . . ."

Hop it!

"All he needs," said the big, bumbly bear, "is a **hug**! Come on, **Scowly-wowly**, give us a cuddle!"

"We just want you to be happy!" the animals cried. But Scowl didn't give a hoot!

"Twit to you!

And **twit** to you too!" he shouted.

Then he flew off to his
Grumpy Branch
for a bit of peace and quiet.
But when he got there . . .

"I AM grumpy!"

screeched the little bird.

"Because YOU broke my HAPPY HAT!"

Scowl felt funny. For the first time
in his life he'd been out-grumped!
    Red-faced, he flapped off and
rescued the happy hat.
Then he gave it to the
little bird and said ...

Grumpy

"Does that hat really make you happy?" asked Scowl. "Yes!" twittered the little bird.

Tee hee

Grumpy Branch

"But what makes you happy, Scowl?" asked the other animals. Scowl had a little think. "Being grumpy!" he said. "It's **great** fun!"

"Yippedy-doodah!" they all cried.
"So we don't need to do anything
to make you happy?"
"Well," said Scowl, "there is
one thing that you could all do."
"What is it?" they asked eagerly.

And they did.

What a hoot!

More hilarious books from Little Tiger Press...

Dr Duck
Steve Smallman • Hannah George

THE GRUNT AND THE GROUCH
Tracey Corderoy • Lee Wildish

Bear's Big Bottom
STEVE SMALLMAN & EMMA YARLETT

Pigeon Poo
Elizabeth Baguley
Mark Chambers

Claire Freedman
Nick East
WHO'S FOR DINNER?

NO!
Tracey Corderoy
Tim Warnes

For information regarding any of the above titles or for our catalogue, please contact us:
Little Tiger Press, 1 The Coda Centre, 189 Munster Road, London SW6 6AW
Tel: 020 7385 6333 • Fax: 020 7385 7333 • E-mail: info@littletiger.co.uk • www.littletiger.co.uk